# TRAPPED BEYOND THE MAGIC ATTIC
by Sheri Cooper Sinykin

Illustrations by
*Gabriel Picart*

Spot Illustrations by
*Rich Grote*

4/8/8

MAGIC ATTIC PRESS

Published by Magic Attic Press.

Copyright © 1997 by MAGIC ATTIC PRESS

Both "tipi" and "tepee" are considered correct spellings of this word. Since "tipi" is
preferred by the Native American community, we use it here.

For more information contact:
Book Editor, Magic Attic Press, 866 Spring Street,
P.O. Box 9722, Portland, ME 04104-5022

First Edition
Printed in the United States of America
1 2 3 4 5 6 7 8 9 10

Magic Attic Club is a registered trademark.

Betsy Gould, Publisher
Marva Martin, Art Director
Jay Brady, Managing Editor

Edited by Judit Bodnar
Designed by Cindy Vacek

**Library of Congress Cataloging·in·Publication Data**
Sinykin, Sheri Cooper.
Trapped Beyond The Magic Attic / by Sheri Cooper Sinykin;
illustrations by Gabriel Picart; spot illustrations by Rich Grote.-- 1st ed.
p. cm. -- ( Magic Attic Club)
Summary: When members of the club and their new friend Rose travel through
the mirror in the magic attic, they become trapped in a natural history museum.

ISBN 1-57513-102-1 (hardcover). -- ISBN 1-57513-101-3 (paperback)
[1. Space and time--Fiction. 2. Museums--Fiction.] I. Picart,
Gabriel, ill. II. Grote, Rich, ill. III. Title. IV. Series.

PZ7.S6194Tr 1997      [Fic]--dc21      97-28005      CIP      AC

As members of the
MAGIC ATTIC CLUB,
we promise to
be best friends,
share all of our adventures in the attic,
use our imaginations,
have lots of fun together,
and remember—the real magic is in us.

*Alison*     *Keisha*

*Heather*     *Megan*

*Rose*

# Table of Contents

# Prologue

When Alison, Heather, Keisha, and Megan find a gold key buried in the snow, they have no idea that it will change their lives forever. They discover that it belongs to Ellie Goodwin, the owner of an old Victorian house across the street from Alison's. Ellie, grateful when they return the key to her, invites the girls to play in her attic. There they find a steamer trunk filled with wonderful outfits—party dresses, a princess gown, a ballet tutu, cowgirl clothes, and many, many, more. Excited, the girls try on some of the costumes and admire their reflections in a tall gilded mirror nearby. Suddenly they are transported to a new time and place, embarking on the greatest adventure of their lives.

When they return to the present and Ellie's attic, they form the Magic Attic Club, promising to tell each other every exciting detail of their future adventures through the mirror.

# Chapter

# One

# TEAMWORK

ecisions, decisions. I wish I weren't team captain," Megan Ryder muttered to herself. With any luck, she'd be able to pick all three of her best friends—Alison McCann, Heather Hardin, and Keisha Vance—before anyone else had a chance to. But in what order should she choose them? Megan hated to hurt anyone's feelings.

"Hurry up, Megan," the gym teacher urged. "We're waiting."

"Let her choose by threes," one of the boys piped up. "It'll go faster."

A couple of kids laughed, but Megan didn't think it was such a bad idea. Apparently, the teacher didn't, either— he was telling the other captains to do just that.

Heather and Keisha stood in front of Alison, the best volleyball server in the class. They crossed their fingers, hoping no one else would call any of their names before Megan did.

Ben Lain started to, but changed his mind.

With a sigh of relief, Megan finally announced, "Alison McCann, Heather Hardin, and Keisha Vance!"

The three girls hurried to line up behind their reddish-blond friend. They whispered suggestions for Megan's final choices.

"Jason's a good spiker," Alison said.

"Yeah," agreed Keisha. "And Mike's fast. He's funny, too."

Heather surveyed their few remaining classmates. "What about the new girl?" she asked, indicating a transfer student with long, dark, straight hair from the private school near the university. "What's her name?"

Alison shrugged, but Keisha said, "Daisy or Rose. Some flower name, I think."

"I hope she's friendlier than she looks," Megan

whispered, "because by the time it's my turn again, she's going to be the only one left."

"Don't worry," Alison said, when Megan's prediction came true. "Once she gets to know us, I'm sure she'll be fine."

Gym class was almost over when Alison's seventh straight service ace moved the team within two points of winning the match. First Megan, then Keisha, then Heather raced back to the serving line to slap palms.

"Come on, Ali," David Jennings called from the net. "Do it again!"

Mike Williams clapped his hands, too. But the new girl just stood there staring. She seemed to be lost in thought.

"Hey!" Alison waved to get the girl's attention. "You ready?"

"The name's Rose, and hay is for horses," the girl shot back.

"Well, excuuuuse me," Alison replied.

"Okay, you guys." Megan turned to the rest of the team. "Let's get these points now!"

Alison served the ball. This time, someone on the other side dove under it just before it hit the floor. Jason jumped at the net, trying to block the return, but the ball

sailed past him. It headed straight to Rose in the center of the court.

"Get it!" the four girls cried. As they did, Megan and Keisha dropped back from the net. Heather and Alison rushed forward. Rose, caught in the middle, made a jump for the ball. She might have hit it, too—if Megan hadn't been in her way.

At the last moment, Keisha stuck her arm out and connected with the ball, sending it up over the net, then down inside the far right corner. Mike and Jason cheered, and the four friends slapped each other on the back.

"Way to go, team!" Megan grinned at her teammates.

"One for all," Alison began.

"And all for one!" Keisha and Heather finished in the same breath. All four giggled. Mike and Jason rolled their eyes. Rose walked away.

Alison noticed and shook her head. She bounced the ball behind the serving line. "Fifteen fourteen. Match point." *Smack*! The ball floated up and seemed to hang above the net. Then suddenly it dropped like a stone just on the other side.

"Wow, Ali!" Heather cried. "That was fantastic!"

"Like magic!" added Keisha.

Alison laughed. "Not really," she said. "But speaking of magic…"

"Shh!" Megan hushed her firmly and gave a quick glance at Rose and the boys. Sometimes it was easy to forget that they weren't alone. Any mention of their secret club would have to wait.

Alison seemed embarrassed. Or maybe, Keisha thought, her cheeks were still flushed from the excitement of the win. It was hard to tell. Alison loved a good contest more than anything—except for their Magic Attic Club adventures.

They were congratulating
each other in the locker room
on their great teamwork when
the bell rang. Rose, trying to
squeeze past Keisha, bumped
her against the wall.

"Ouch!" Keisha rubbed her
elbow. "All you had to do was
ask me to move, Rose."

"Hey—you remembered my
name." The girl mumbled
something else, then hurried
away.

Keisha and the others stared after her. Megan shook
her head and said, "Isn't she the one who said, 'Hay is for
horses'? Boy, who does she think she is anyway?"

"Yeah," Alison chimed in. "Just because she went to
some fancy private school."

Heather said nothing. Because her father was a pilot,
her family had moved around a lot. She'd often been the
new girl herself. Luckily for her, she'd met Alison, Keisha,
and Megan. Still, she thought, Rose could have tried
harder, or at least said she was sorry.

Chapter

## Two

# A SURPRISE AT ELLIE'S

lison rang her next-door neighbor's doorbell one last time. Keisha, Heather, and Megan pressed close, stomping their boots on Ellie Goodwin's porch and blowing on their bare hands. "I'm sure she's home," Alison said. "The light's on."

Megan glanced at her watch. "Maybe she's busy. Let's come back later."

"No, wait," Keisha said. "She's coming."

The door to the white Victorian house swung wide.

"I thought I heard the bell." Ellie smiled at
the girls and invited them inside.

A pair of half-glasses hung from
a gold chain around Ellie's neck.
"Are those new?" Heather asked.

The older woman nodded. "I
need them when I use my computer."
At the girls' surprised expressions, she
added, "Didn't I tell you I'd ordered one? Come see."

The girls hung their coats in the closet, kicked off their
boots, and followed Ellie to the study. Sitting at the
keyboard was a dark-haired girl dressed in a green plaid
jumper. A green tam and a denim purse adorned with a
beaded design hung behind her on the chair.

Keisha stopped short, causing the other girls to run
into her from behind. "Are you teaching computer now,
too?" she asked. Ellie was a voice and piano teacher as
well; there seemed to be no end to the things she was
good at.

"Goodness no!" Ellie laughed lightly. "This time I'm the
student. We're designing Christmas cards."

"Cool," said Heather. "Who's your teach—" she began
to ask. But when the girl at the computer swiveled her
chair around, Heather almost choked on the word.

"Do you girls know Rose Hopkins?" Ellie asked.

Their heads bobbed mechanically. Megan looked at the other girls. They looked stunned to see Rose there, too. She seemed to be everywhere they were!

"Well," said Alison, "we don't want to interrupt or anything. Is it okay if we go up to the attic?"

"We, um, play up there sometimes." Keisha wasn't sure why she felt the need to explain.

"Well," Rose said, "we're playing down here, too, aren't we, Ellie?"

"Maybe you are," Ellie replied lightly. "Unfortunately, it still feels like work to me." Turning back to the computer screen, she sat down beside Rose and waved the girls off to the attic.

The girls picked up the key to the attic from the table in the front hall. Megan led the way upstairs, her friends following close behind. "I never expected to find *her* at Ellie's," she said.

"Me, either." Alison pulled the cord on the lamp that hung from the ceiling. A warm glow welcomed them to their favorite meeting place.

The girls sat cross-legged in a circle on the oriental carpet. Not one of them even looked in the direction of the huge steamer trunk that held the beginnings of all their adventures. Seeing Rose with Ellie had somehow spoiled everything.

"So," Keisha began, "here we all are."

"We could plan a party," suggested Heather. "'Tis the season,' and all that." She smiled hopefully.

"A party just for us, right?" Megan asked.

"And Ellie," Alison said. "We can't forget her."

Keisha played with one of her braids. "You know," she said at last, "it wouldn't kill us to invite Rose, too."

"Keisha!" the other three chorused.

"I mean it. Maybe she's not that bad. Maybe we got the wrong impression."

"I know I did—about you guys," Heather said, a bit hesitantly.

"And what's that supposed to mean?" Keisha looked wounded.

Heather's cheeks burned. The girls seemed to take their friendship for granted, but she was still keenly aware of how grateful she felt to finally belong. "Well," she started slowly, struggling to put the best spin on her memories. "Take Megan for instance. At first it seemed like she'd rather read a book than talk to me."

"Me?" Megan jumped to her feet. "What about you, always bragging about what a great dancer you are!"

"I wasn't bragging," Heather replied. "Alison's the one, always showing off her sports trophies."

"I thought you guys wanted to see them," Alison said.

"Not all of them." Keisha rolled her eyes. "And not all the time."

"Well, thanks for telling me," Alison fumed. "It's nice to know who my friends are." She turned away, and an uneasy silence settled over the attic.

At last Keisha spoke. "Look, this is crazy. We're friends. Best friends. Why are we fighting, anyway?"

Megan and Alison both looked accusingly at Heather, who hung her head.

"All she meant was that sometimes we get the wrong idea about people," Keisha said. "Including each other."

Heather gave her a small smile of gratitude. "Really," she added, "I didn't mean to get everybody all mad."

"So, truce, okay? Let's shake on it." Keisha tugged on each girl's hand until all four met in the middle of the circle.

"Does this mean we're going to try again with Rose?" Heather asked.

"It's okay with me," Megan said.

"Come on, then. Let's go talk to her." Keisha scrambled to her feet before the others could change their minds.

Downstairs, however, they found Ellie alone at the computer, staring intently at the screen.

When the girls drew closer, they saw that she was playing Solitaire.

"Where's Rose?" asked Heather.

Ellie gasped as she spun around. "Girls! You scared the daylights right out of me!"

"Sorry, Ellie, " Megan said. "We didn't mean to."

Ellie nodded. "It's too bad Rose had to leave. I was hoping you might all be friends."

"I guess we kind of got off on the wrong foot with her at school," Alison said, speaking for them all. "We were going to talk to her. That's why we came down here."

Megan and Heather gave Ellie an apologetic shrug. Keisha picked up one of the Christmas cards. "Rose did this all by herself? Amazing."

Ellie nodded. "The girl has quite a mind for computers, that's for sure." She looked as if she wanted to say something more but thought better of it.

Keisha turned to the others. "Wouldn't it be cool to make our own cards?"

"Do you think Rose would help us?" Alison wondered aloud.

"After the way we treated her?" Heather shook her head.

"I'd be too embarrassed to even ask," added Megan.

Ellie smiled sympathetically. "It never hurts to try again."

Keisha looked at the others. No one spoke.

"Well," Ellie said, turning back to her Solitaire game, "she's coming by after school tomorrow, if you change your minds."

# Chapter
# *Three*

# SOMETHING NEW IN THE ATTIC

 ose was teaching Ellie how to design her own stationery when the four girls showed up again the next day. Why were they always coming around, Rose wondered. She faced the screen, wishing she could hit the DELETE key and make them disappear.

"Hi, Rose," Keisha said, plunking herself down in Ellie's chair.

Ali herded the others closer until

they were all standing right behind the computer, breathing down Rose's neck. Rose couldn't help fidgeting.

"Looks like you're done with the cards," said Heather. "What're you doing now?"

Rose pursed her lips. Were they looking for some way to make fun of her, or were they really interested? "I just finished customizing Ellie's database, and now we're designing a letterhead." She fully expected the girls' eyes to glaze over. Instead, they asked questions, and even more surprising, paid attention to her replies.

"How'd you learn all those things?" Megan's voice was soft with awe. "I read a lot, but somehow computer books never make much sense. Not to me, anyway."

"My parents say it's a gift." Rose shrugged. "Maybe it is. But I'm sure it helps to go to the university's computer camp and private school and stuff."

"I guess so," Alison said. "We hardly even get to use the computers at our school."

Keisha nudged Megan and wondered whether they shared the same thought: Rose probably knew way more than the so-called media specialist who was trying to put together a computer lab in the library.

"What else do you know about computers?" Keisha asked.

Rose hesitated. What did they want from her? "You

really want to know?" She looked from one girl to the other. They all seemed genuinely interested in her reply. "Well, I made a home page on the internet. And I've been working on this game. It's about some kids and their adventures. They're in this club, and they build this computer that actually sends them into cyberspace. With the right password, they can go wherever they want to. Back in time or into the future, even."

Alison elbowed Megan and raised one eyebrow. Bet she's right for the Magic Attic Club, she seemed to be saying.

Megan nodded, and glancing at Rose and then up toward the attic, silently asked Keisha and Heather. Their response made it unanimous.

Rose was still explaining her computer game when Alison interrupted. "Excuse me. Ellie, could I talk to you for a minute in the other room?"

Rose clammed up immediately. She'd said too much, she decided. No doubt the girls were going to go play without her again, just like the day before.

Heather sensed Rose's uneasiness. But she knew it would disappear just as soon as Ali asked Ellie's permission to take Rose up to the attic.

At the girls' invitation, Rose hesitated, unsure what to

make of it. They all seemed awfully excited. What was so fascinating about playing in an attic?

"I promise you, dear," Ellie said, "you'll have the time of your life. Run along. Mr. Megabytes and I will be fine."

At that, Rose grinned. "Okay. If you say so."

Alison took the scrolled key from the silver-lidded box on the table in the hall. "Thanks, Ellie," she said. "We'll be back soon."

Rose frowned. "You make it sound like we're going on a trip or something."

"Don't worry." Keisha put her arm around Rose's shoulder. "We'll explain everything." On the way upstairs, she and Heather exchanged a knowing smile.

Rose wondered what they looked so pleased about. Poking around somebody else's dusty old attic hardly seemed the height of entertainment. Maybe the girls were helping Ellie find some old music or books she'd packed away up there.

When she saw what awaited her in the attic, Rose raised her eyebrows in surprise. There was a tall, gilded mirror flanked by a wardrobe and antique desk, a lush oriental rug, and an old steamer trunk heaped with colorful outfits.

The whole room had an old-fashioned cedar-and-mothballs smell that reminded Rose of her favorite great-aunt's guest room. "What do you do up here?" she asked. "Play dress-up?"

"Better than that," replied Megan. "You know that computer game you were telling us about? Well, we go on our own adventures."

Rose was impressed. She grudgingly admitted to herself that perhaps they had some imagination.

"It all started when we found Ellie's key in the snow," Heather started to explain. One by one, Keisha, Megan, and Alison jumped in, adding more details about Ellie inviting them to visit the attic and the girls' first adventure through the gilded mirror.

"We went back to the 1930s," Alison said, "and even I wore a dress."

"You time-traveled?" Rose's eyes grew wide. "I can't believe it."

"Not only that," Megan chimed in, "but we met Ellie when she was our age."

"But that's impossible—isn't it?" Rose looked from one girl to the other, but they all seemed to believe the story.

"Look," Keisha said, "the clothes we wore are in here somewhere." Alison, Heather and Megan all began to

search through the jumble of outfits. Soon their delighted squeals seemed to charge the air with a kind of electricity.

Rose drew closer. She watched expectantly as the girls pulled out the very same party dresses they had described. Heather surfaced from the trunk last, with not one but two dresses. Rose grinned at the sight of the first. The bodice was forest green velvet, trimmed at the collar and cuffs with white lace. The skirt was a swishy, rustling plaid.

"You like this one? Good!" Heather handed it to Rose. "I can't find mine, but I like this even better. Don't you?" she asked the others, holding up a red velvet dress trimmed in rich gold. Keisha, Alison, and Megan murmured approvingly.

"So," Rose said, "let me get this right. If we try these on and all look in the mirror, we'll be whisked away on some amazing adventure?"

"That's what's happened every other time," Keisha replied.

"But how does it work? I don't understand."

Alison sighed. "Look. Think of it the way my mom thinks of microwave ovens. She doesn't understand them, doesn't know how they work. She just trusts that they will, when she follows the directions."

"Come on," Megan urged. "It'll be great. Would we lie to you?"

I hope not, Rose thought as she changed into the fancy green dress, and she and the other girls all held hands and approached the mirror.

# Chapter Four

# A STRANGE DISAPPEARANCE

migosh!" Heather gasped. "Look at that!" Before her stood the largest indoor Christmas tree she'd ever seen. Simple gold ornaments and woven floral ropes adorned its fragrant branches. "It must be twenty feet tall!"

Keisha, Megan, and Alison stared in awe. Rose, however,

stayed close to Heather and glanced nervously at everything *but* the tree: at the polished marble floor that stretched out before them; at the massive dinosaur skeleton that loomed behind; at the crowd of well-dressed children who surrounded them, eating cookies and drinking punch.

"You guys," Rose said, finding her voice at last, "w-w-where are we?"

"I'm not sure yet," Alison replied. "But don't worry. Figuring it out is half the fun."

"You're sure?"

"Absolutely." Keisha and Megan spoke as one.

Heather realized that she and the others had become so used to going through the attic mirror that they'd forgotten how unsettling their first adventure had been. No wonder Rose stood frozen beside her. "Come on," she said. "Just act like we belong."

Red and green balloons made an archway over the refreshment table. A banner said WELCOME TO THE NATURAL HISTORY MUSEUM HOLIDAY OPEN HOUSE. Helping themselves to some cookies, the girls mingled with the other children.

WELCOME
to the
NATURAL HISTORY
MUSEUM
HOLIDAY
OPEN HOUSE

"Well," Megan whispered to Rose, "now we know where we are."

"That's what it says, but I'm still not sure I believe my eyes," Rose answered. "This is so—incredible!"

Mounted on a fat marble pillar was an arrow pointing left to displays of bird habitats, reptiles, and mammal fossils. To the right were more dinosaurs, along with plants of the world, and something called a nature walk.

Rose sighed. Maybe the culture exhibits were upstairs. It would only take a minute to check the directory. "Stay here, you guys, okay?" she said. "I'll be right back." Without waiting for a reply, she took off.

"This is so cool," Keisha said. "I want to go explore, don't you?"

Heather nodded. "Gems of the world, that's what I want to see."

"Not me." Megan shook her head. "Isn't there a Planet Ocean display around here?"

"That's like an aquarium, right?" Alison looked around. "I'm sure it's here somewhere. But let's go check out the dinosaur stuff first. It's right over there."

"And the bird gallery is just over there." Keisha pointed in the opposite direction.

"Birds!" Alison rolled her eyes. "You can see those any old time, Keish."

"Why don't we split up?" suggested Heather. "I could go with Keisha, and Megan could go with you, Ali."

"Good idea. It'd save time." Megan glanced about. "Hey—where did Rose go?"

"Here she comes." Keisha waved as their new friend approached.

The party crowd was starting to thin out. The girls would be able to zip through the exhibits in no time.

Rose's cheeks were flushed and her eyes seemed to hint at some exciting discovery. "You guys, I've got to show you something. It's exactly as Grandfather described it."

"Later," Alison said. "We've got it all decided." She motioned for Megan to follow her.

Rose pressed her lips together, trying to hide her disappointment. "You two come, then," she said to Heather and Keisha. Certain that they would follow her, she headed for the stairs.

Alison stared at the eighty-foot-long skeleton of *Diplodocus*. The sign said it was the largest animal ever to have walked the earth. "Isn't it weird how something this big could just disappear?" she asked Megan.

Megan looked up from the brochure she'd found on the floor. "It's unbelievable, when you think about it."

"Sheesh, Megan," Alison teased, "you'll read anything, won't you?"

Megan grinned. "Never know what might come in handy."

"Did you find Planet Ocean?"

"Not yet. I was just—"

"The Natural History Museum will be closing in

ten minutes," a voice over the loudspeaker began. "Please proceed to the nearest exit immediately."

"Uh-oh." Megan grabbed Alison's hand. "Come on. We've got to go find the others."

"Don't worry. We've got ten whole minutes," Alison said. "And besides, I know exactly where they are." She pointed to the other first-floor gallery. "As long as we stick together, what could go wrong?"

On the other side of the museum, Keisha and Heather were admiring the colored gemstones from Brazil and having the same conversation about meeting up with the other girls. "But I think we should wait here," Heather said, "and let them find us."

Keisha disagreed. "They're probably waiting by the

balloons, right where we left them."

Heather bit her lip. How many minutes were they wasting? What if Alison and Megan were still in the dinosaur hall, expecting the others to go get *them*? She suggested this to Keisha.

"If we had a coin, we could flip it." Keisha grinned halfheartedly.

"And if we had a mirror," replied Heather, "we could go home."

"What, and miss our adventure?" Keisha laughed nervously. "Come on. We're wasting time just standing here."

To their great relief, as they hurried toward the towering Christmas tree, Alison and Megan approached from the opposite direction. After exchanging quick hugs, the four girls looked around. Concern lined their faces as the realization struck: Rose most definitely was nowhere to be found.

# Five

# TRAPPED!

h, great." Keisha sighed and glanced around. She and her friends seemed to be the only ones left in the gallery. "Now what do we do? The museum's closing any minute."

"I know," Megan said, "but we've got to find Rose. Does anybody know where she could have gone?"

"Probably to some exhibit her grandfather told her about," replied Alison. "I should have gone with her, I guess, but I—"

"Don't blame yourself, Ali." Heather patted her arm. "We all could have gone—or at least listened to what she was saying."

"Let's start upstairs," Keisha suggested. "If she was down here, at least one of us would have seen her by now, don't you think?"

The other girls nodded and paired up. After consulting the directory at the foot of the stairs, Megan and Alison decided to search the second floor's east wing, where Planet Ocean was located. Keisha and Heather would search among the Native Peoples displays in the west wing.

"Okay, here's the plan," Alison said. "Do a quick search of your area, and when you find her, meet back here."

As they set out, their footsteps tapped out a crazy beat that seemed to echo throughout the deserted museum.

At the top of the stairs, Heather stopped short. "What if the museum closes first?" she asked. "I mean, before we can all meet up again?"

Alison frowned. They'd never before gone back through the mirror without first having had an adventure. But what if they got caught? Surely a guard would want to call their parents—maybe even the police! That could be a problem, since they hadn't figured out yet what city they were in—or for that matter, what year.

"If that happens," Alison said at last, "maybe we'd better go through the mirror with whoever we're with. The main thing is, we can't get caught.

There's no way we could explain how we got here. Deal?" She put out her hand and the others shook it in turn, sealing the agreement.

Without warning, the overhead lights blinked and went out. All that lighted Megan's and Alison's way now was an eerie glow from a nearby aquarium. A strange sound, something between a click and a chirp, came from somewhere in Planet Ocean.

Megan clutched at her friend's hand. "What's that?"

"I-I don't know."

"Some kind of creature?"

"If it is," Alison said, "then it better be behind glass."

Megan nodded, her eyes wide. Together they tiptoed farther into what seemed to be a tunnel windowed with aquariums. There was no sign of Rose.

At last the dark corridor opened onto a circular room containing a huge fish tank. Lights above the water gave off a pale green glow. The clicking sound grew louder. Alison looked up to see several audio speakers mounted on the wall.

Megan, in the meantime, squinted to make out what the sign said. "Whew! We can relax," she whispered. "That sound—that's just the dolphins talking."

Suddenly, from somewhere on the other side of the tank came the jangle of keys, followed by footsteps. At the thought of their being caught by a guard, Megan froze.

Alison, on the other hand, scanned the gloom for a hiding place. She spotted a crawl space under the observation platform. She mouthed the words "Follow me" to Megan, then ducked under the restraining rope. In an instant, Megan was beside her, and the two girls squirmed on their bellies into the dusty hollow.

The footsteps came closer. Megan held her breath and prayed that she wouldn't sneeze. Her heart was pounding so hard, she was sure whoever it was could hear her.

"Good. He's finally gone." Alison unloosed the breath she'd been holding. "Come on. Let's get out of here."

"Back to the stairs, right?" Megan said. "We promised."

Alison nodded. The two crept out of hiding and tiptoed back through the aquatic exhibit. But as they approached the area where the east wing met the west, a security gate blocked their way. And though the stairs were on the other side, Heather, Keisha, and Rose were not.

"Quick," Alison said, not giving herself or Megan time to panic. "Check the map. Where's the nearest bathroom? We've got to get to a mirror."

Megan's hands trembled as she unfolded the museum brochure. "Back that way." She pointed over her shoulder. "Come on."

Like an expert trail guide, Megan dragged Alison past Planet Ocean and through the mazelike Evolution display beyond it. At the sight of little booths with "Touch Me" computer terminals, she took a moment to search each one, half expecting to find Rose. Dumb, Megan chided herself. Computers needed power, and the museum was obviously not wasting any, now that it was closed.

At last, in the back corner of the east wing, Megan found the women's restroom. There was no door, only an archway, and around the corner, almost total darkness. With their movement, however, a light snapped on. Grateful, the girls rushed over to the long mirror.

"I-I feel like we're ditching them," Megan whispered.

"I know. Me, too. But they probably did the same thing, once they saw we were cut off."

Megan nodded and took Alison's hand. Both girls gazed at their reflections, then closed their eyes.

Nothing happened.

"Oh, no!" Megan pressed her lips together. She tried to remain calm. "It doesn't work."

"Let's try again," whispered Alison.

But Megan shook her head. "I bet it's because we're not all together."

"If that's true," Alison said, "then the others are still here, too. But how are we going to get to them? It seems like we're all trapped."

Trapped beyond the mirror! Megan's heart raced almost as fast as her thoughts. Then a sudden rumbling noise outside made her jump.

Alison rushed toward the entrance. She arrived just in time to see a security gate roll swiftly across the opening, blocking their escape. "Omigosh, Megan, look! Now we really are trapped!"

Chapter
## Six

# ESCAPE AND DISCOVERY

anic rose in Megan's chest, but she forced it back and cleared her mind. She glanced around the bathroom at the low ceiling and the old-fashioned windows. Would an alarm go off if she opened one? What was on the other side? A fire escape, maybe?

"Ali, let's try the window," she suggested.

Alison raised the sash, then stuck her head outside to investigate. Not only was there a fire escape, there was a narrow catwalk that seemed to link it to another one off the west wing.

"Megan, check this out, and let me see the map, will you?" Alison studied the museum floor plan. It confirmed her hope that the other fire escape was right outside the west wing bathroom. I bet Heather, Keisha, and Rose are stuck in there right now, she said to herself. All she and Megan had to do was walk across and

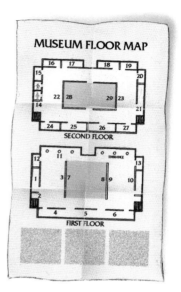

knock on the window. They were as good as home.

Keisha checked the last bathroom stall, then sighed. "I was so sure she'd be in here."

"I know. I think we checked everywhere else, didn't we?" Heather asked.

"Everywhere but the Plains Indians exhibit."

"All right," Keisha replied. "But if Rose is not there, then we go meet the others. She's probably with them."

As they turned to leave, a sudden frantic knocking at the window made them jump and spin around. A girl's silhouette was plainly visible. Could it be Rose?

Keisha raised the window. But it was Alison who

climbed inside, followed moments later by Megan. "What in the world?" Keisha and Heather said, almost in unison.

"See, Megan? Didn't I tell you they'd be here?" Alison grinned triumphantly, then hugged her bewildered friends. She and Megan wasted no time in filling the others in on their unsuccessful try to go home through the mirror, as well as on their brief imprisonment.

"Well," Heather said, "at least *we're* not locked in. Not yet anyway. But we still need to find Rose."

"Come on, then." Alison hurried the others through the open doorway, half expecting another security gate to appear at any moment. She was surprised to discover that in this wing, at least, the lights were still on.

"This way," Keisha whispered. "We think we know where she might be."

The janitor's supply cart squeaked away down the long hall. At last, Rose sneaked out of the Cheyenne tipi, taking great care not to bump anything in the diorama. She'd gotten herself into a real fix this time, expecting all the other girls to go where she wanted to go. What did she think they were, puppets she could move around a stage simply by writing the script? No wonder they'd gone off and left her.

Still, Rose chided herself for having trusted them. A

great adventure, they'd said. Ha. What was she going to do now? No guard was going to believe how she'd gotten there, that was for sure. She had best rely on herself.

"Pssst! Rose!"

Turning with a start, Rose saw the four girls rushing toward her.

"You didn't think we'd leave without you, did you?" whispered Heather.

"I hoped not," Rose said. "But I guess I didn't exactly make things easy, taking off the way I did. Sorry."

"Is this what you wanted to show us?" asked Keisha, indicating the diorama of a scene from Cheyenne daily life. Outside the tipi, a woman was using a bone "flesher" to scrape meat from a buffalo hide. A little boy was fashioning a sled out of the same animal's ribs. Nearby, a girl played with a deerskin doll.

As she studied the diorama, Keisha thought she saw Rose's expression soften. "Are you Cheyenne?" she asked at last.

No need to take offense or look for an insult, Rose thought. Keisha's simply interested, that's all. "Yes," she replied. "My grandfather posed as a model for a display like this when he was a little boy."

The other girls came closer to look at the lifelike faces. "Is that one him?" Megan asked.

Rose shrugged. "Could be. It's hard to tell."

"That's so cool," Alison said. "He must have lots of great stories."

"Oh, he does. And it's a good thing I never get tired of hearing them."

"Why's that?" asked Keisha.

Rose grinned. "Because he lives with us."

"Well, maybe we'll get to meet him sometime," Megan said. "But first we have to get home. Come on! Take your shoes off so we don't make any noise."

Racing around the bend in their stocking feet, the girls followed Alison, who whispered hoarsely over her shoulder, "Last one to the bathroom mirror is a rotten egg!"

But at the end of the hall, they slid to a halt. Another security gate blocked the doorway.

"Oh, no," Megan moaned. "Not again."

Alison pressed her hand to her forehead. Who ever said the third time was the charm, she wondered to herself. "Wait, you guys," she finally said. "Maybe we can still get down the stairs. I think they're only blocked from the other wing."

"She's right." Megan whipped the museum brochure out again, glad she'd ignored Alison's teasing about picking it up in the first place. "There's one more bathroom we could try down there."

"Well, we'd better hurry," Heather said, "before they block that one, too."

Still carrying their shoes, the girls hustled after Alison. As they hit the marble stairs, all the remaining lights in the museum blinked off, even the ones from the Christmas tree, as if they hit a switch—or someone else did. Could someone be watching them? Alison wondered with a shiver.

They sock-skated across the first floor, brushing past the columns of balloons. Only the green glow of exit signs pierced the dark. After stopping to slip their shoes back on, the girls grabbed each other's hands and shuffled cautiously forward toward where Megan figured the bathroom would be.

But they could already see that the gate was down.

"Does anybody have any brainy ideas?" asked Alison.

For a long moment, no one spoke. From somewhere above them, the squeak of the custodian's cart grated through the air like fingernails on a chalkboard.

"Think! *Think!*" whispered Heather.

"I don't know," Rose said. "Maybe this won't work, but—"

"What? Tell us!" Keisha urged.

"Well, there's got to be a control room around here somewhere," she reasoned. "And maybe, if I can get to the computer, I can bring up the security program and—"

"Oh, right," Alison interrupted. "Like a kid our age could just walk in there and do that."

"But she's a computer brainiac," Heather cut in. "Aren't you, Rose? If she says she can do it, then I say we go for it. Unless someone else has a better idea."

No one volunteered anything, and Megan finally suggested that they try to get to the lower level. "That's where the brochure says the offices are, anyway."

"The basement is where the hospital's computer room is," whispered Keisha. "I saw it one time, when I was there with my dad."

Huddling together, they moved back toward the stairs. "If we run into anybody," Heather said, "you do the talking, okay, Megan?"

The marble stairs were slick and smelled faintly of some kind of cleaning solution. "Hold on to the rail," Alison warned the other girls, her voice low. "Come on."

Megan tried to remember what was where on the

lowest level. There wasn't enough light to read the brochure. And there wasn't enough time to simply wander around and hope they'd get lucky. On this adventure, luck was the last thing they could count on.

Suddenly Keisha clutched the hand nearest hers. "Listen, you guys." Men's voices were coming from somewhere to the right of them. She strained to figure out whether they were getting louder.

"Quick," Megan said. "Under the stairs."

The girls rushed to their hiding place. A few moments later, the voices faded. At least for the time being, the girls were all right.

"Come on," Rose said. "We've got to find that computer."

"Turn left," Megan said. "I think this'll lead to the offices."

Soon, the strong aroma of coffee and a constant, low humming sound filled the air, which had abruptly become cooler. "I bet we're getting close." Rose sounded excited, as if her fingers were itching to touch a keyboard again. "See? Around the bend, there's some kind of light."

"Should we all go?" Megan asked. "Or should we send out a scout?"

"And I suppose that means me, right? Because I'm the Indian?" Though Rose kept her voice low, there was no mistaking its sarcastic edge.

"Don't be so touchy," Keisha cut in. "Megan's not like that."

"It's just an expression, Rose," Megan said.

# Chapter Seven

# ALL FOR ONE

 e don't have time for this," Heather interrupted, plainly exasperated. "We have to work together."

"You're right." Keisha turned to Rose. "I'm sorry. I shouldn't have jumped on you."

"I guess I was being touchy," Rose admitted. "'Paper-skinned,' Grandfather calls it. I can get like that."

Keisha nodded. Sometimes, when she thought people were making ignorant comments about her being African-American, she felt that way herself. No doubt Heather had similar experiences being Jewish.

"Never mind. I'll scout it out," whispered Megan, ending the discussion. Before anyone could argue, she was tiptoeing down the corridor toward the lighted window.

The other girls stayed behind, peering around the corner. If Megan did get caught, she'd at least know how to talk their way out of trouble, Alison assured herself.

Moments later, Megan returned, breathless. "The computer's in there, all right," she said. "And so is a guard."

"Only one?" asked Alison.

Megan nodded. "The door appears to be locked, but I could see through the window."

"What else did you see?" Keisha pressed closer.

"There's some kind of classroom across the hall," Megan replied. "That door is open, at least. If we could just distract the guard, get him out of that room somehow..."

"How long would you need, Rose?" Heather asked.

"It depends. If we're lucky, only a couple of minutes."

Alison snapped her fingers softly. "I've got an idea! If we all do our part, we just might get out of here."

Across the hall from the computer room, Heather, Keisha, and Rose huddled together behind the open door. From that position, all three could get a glimpse of the guard through the space near the hinges. He was reading a book, a thick paperback. Some watchman he was! Would he even notice what Alison and Megan were about to do? Any minute, they would be in position. The rest had to go like clockwork.

As they waited, poised to make a run for the computer room, each girl was alone with her thoughts. Keisha worried about the door. What if it snapped shut behind the guard before they could sneak inside? Some of the doors at her father's hospital were rigged to close that way. Fast. With a whoosh.

Heather wondered whether Rose really knew as much about computers as she led them all to believe. Even if she did, what were her nerves like? What if she came totally unglued?

Rose thought about the fact that her new friends were counting on her. But a million things could go wrong. She could be locked out of the system, or it could freeze. There wouldn't be enough time to crack a password. It was one thing to know how to do all these things in theory, and another to do them under pressure, with people standing over you.

Bang! Bang! Bang! The sounds came from down the hall, to the left.

"Okay, get ready," Keisha whispered.

The guard looked up from his book. A frown crossed his face.

Bang! Bang! The sounds were closer, but to the right.

Now the guard was on his feet, heading toward the door. The knob turned. Across the hall, Keisha crouched, ready to spring into action.

The guard emerged, glanced quickly up and down the corridor, then drew something from his hip. Rose, fearing it might be a gun, clutched at Keisha, holding her back. But she saw it was only a flashlight and started breathing again. Its beam raced ahead of the man as he took off down the hall.

Just before he flipped the corridor's lights on, Keisha dove for the doorway, wedging one arm between the jamb and the fast-closing door. She waved Heather and Rose across and quickly angled the mini blinds so no one could see inside. Then she latched the door.

Rose took a seat and slid the keyboard out. Heather stood behind her, watching the monitor, while Keisha listened at the door.

Bang! Bang! Bang!

"Those bursting balloons really do sound scary,"

Keisha whispered. "Like firecrackers or gunshots or something."

Heather nodded. "They echo like crazy, too."

"That was a great idea for Megan and Ali to divide up the whole arch and run all over the place popping them. That poor guy must be so confused."

"Shhhh!" Rose hissed. "How do you expect me to concentrate with you jabbering like crows?" It wasn't going to be easy to break the security of this computer, she thought, even without distractions.

Heather and Keisha apologized and fell silent. Even the soft *clickety-clickety-click* of the keyboard grated on their nerves. Rose seemed to be talking to herself, thinking out loud, maybe. What if they all had overestimated her skills?

"Ha!" Rose exclaimed. "Look at this!"

Detailed floor plans of the museum appeared on the screen.

"See these red blinking lines?" Rose pointed them out quickly. "I think they're the security gates that are already in place."

"Turn them off!" Keisha said. "Can you do that?"

"I'm trying." Rose's fingers flew over the keys. Each time she hit ENTER, however, a window popped up that said ACCESS DENIED.

"I'll go check the hall," Heather offered. She raised one of the blinds. No one was coming—not yet, anyway. It sounded like Megan and Alison were leading the guard on a wild-goose chase. They did have a map, after all. Heather hoped that with Megan's sense of direction and Alison's speed, they'd be successful in eluding the guard.

"It won't let me in!" Rose's voice was high and tight. "I need more time!"

"Take a deep breath and try to relax," Keisha said. "There's an answer here somewhere. We've just got to be cool."

"Okay, okay." With her mouse, Rose highlighted the corridor in which the computer room was located. Then somehow she managed to bring up an enlarged view that showed more detail. "Here's where we meet Alison and Megan, right?"

Keisha nodded quickly. Under the stairs had seemed like a great meeting place when they'd set it up. From there, they could go in three different directions if they had to, to avoid being caught.

Heather closed the blinds and peered at the computer screen. "Omigosh! Rose, look!" Heather's finger trembled as she pointed out a locker room just behind the stairway.

Keisha leaned in closer. "There's no red line there, right?"

"Uh, right," Rose said, annoyed that she hadn't noticed it herself. "All we'd have to do is just walk in."

"And there's bound to be a mirror in a locker room," Keisha said.

"Rose, you did it!" Heather slapped her on the back.

Rose blushed. "Actually, *we* did it," she said.

"Let's not celebrate yet," Keisha cut in. "When was the last time you heard any balloons?"

Rose and Heather stared at each other, then at Keisha. Their eyes grew wide. "Oh, no! They must be out of ammo," Heather said.

Keisha grabbed their hands and practically dragged them out of the room and toward the stairs. They slid across the marble floor and dove for shelter, their hearts beating fast.

Footsteps echoed overhead, coming closer.

# Chapter
## Eight

# ROSE'S IDEA

eather, Keisha, and Rose pressed closer together in the dark hollow beneath the stairs. No one spoke or even seemed to breathe.

Suddenly, there was a swishing sound right in front of them, followed by hands groping the air. "You guys, it's us!" Megan whispered.

Keisha reached out and pulled her and Alison into the hiding place.

"We've got to get out of here!" Alison's words tumbled

out in a rush. "He's right behind us!"

"This way! Hurry!" Heather grabbed Alison's hand.

Rose took Megan's hand, and Keisha led the way to the locker room. In their haste, the girls forgot to take their shoes off. Their heels clattered noisily on the marble floor. Keys jangled somewhere behind them. A flashlight's beam danced along the walls.

"Hey! Stop!" a man's voice called.

Keisha's heart raced as she leaned hard on the locker room door. It swung open soundlessly, and the other girls surged in behind her. A light sensed their presence and snapped on overhead. Two aisles of lockers stretched before them. At the end was a full-length mirror.

"Come on!" Megan cried.

The five friends reached the mirror in the same instant, held hands, and made the same wish. The last thing any of them heard was the guard saying, "I could have sworn I saw a bunch of little girls go in here a second ago…"

Rose blinked in amazement. Just as the girls had promised, they were all safely back in Ellie Goodwin's attic. She saw the steamer trunk, the huge mahogany wardrobe, and the tall gilded mirror. She stared at her reflection and let her heartbeat return to normal.

The other girls were changing into their regular

clothes, so Rose did, too. No one was talking, though, and she wondered whether she could have imagined the whole incredible adventure. "Well," she finally said, looking around hesitantly, "thank you for—um, inviting me." Not knowing what else to do, she turned to leave.

"Rose, wait. Don't go." Heather rushed toward her. In an instant, the others were all laughing and talking at once.

"Did you have a good time?"

"Are you glad you went?"

"Which part did you like best?"

Rose grinned, letting the feeling of togetherness surround her. "It was fantastic," she said. "Really unbelievable. Where else have you gone?"

The others all tried to talk at once: Edwardian England, Africa, a wedding, to rescue a unicorn.

"Whoa!" Rose laughed. "One at a time."

Her eyes grew wide as Heather, Megan, Keisha, and Alison took turns telling her all about their adventures in Ellie's attic and how they'd formed the Magic Attic Club.

"Our only rule," Alison said, "is that we have to promise to tell each other all about any adventure we take through the mirror."

"We were going to write them up in an official club notebook," Keisha said.

"But what would happen if somebody else—some grown-up—got a hold of it?" Rose asked, concerned.

"That's the problem," Alison replied. "So far, we just write in our own diaries."

Rose nodded and fell silent.

Heather cleared her throat, almost shyly. "It's so cool they way you braid ribbons in your hair, Rose," she said. "Maybe sometime you could show us how."

"Oh, would you?" Megan's face lit up at the thought.

"Sure!" Rose grinned. "We could sit in a circle, even, and all do each other's hair at the same time."

"At a sleepover," Keisha crowed.

"Anywhere but at my house," added Alison. "Too many brothers."

Rose hesitated. "How about mine?"

The other girls nodded in agreement.

"Cool. I'll ask my mom." The glow from the attic lamp seemed to reflect how Rose felt inside. As much as she loved cooking special dinners with her grandfather or teaching her pet cockatiel to speak, going with the girls on this adventure beat everything. It was no contest. If only she could program this moment into her computer and replay it whenever she wanted to!

Megan searched the other girls' faces, taking an unspoken vote. "So, Rose," she said at last, "do you want to be an official member of the Magic Attic Club, too?"

"You really mean it?" Rose looked from one girl to the other. Their answer was clear. "I'd love to!" she cried.

"Hey, Rose." Heather cringed as soon as the words were out of her mouth. "Sorry. Hay is for horses, right?"

Rose laughed and waved away Heather's concern. "'Hey, Rose,' what?"

"Do you think you could teach us some special stuff on the computer?" Heather asked uncertainly. "Like you were teaching Ellie?"

Rose grinned broadly. "Sure. It'll be fun. I'll make you all experts in no time."

Alison grabbed the attic key from the desk. "Then it's all settled. Let's go tell Ellie—she'll be really glad." She clapped an arm around Rose's shoulder. Heather, Keisha, and Megan fell in alongside, filling the hallway. The new Magic Attic Club was on its way.